大大大大
的鱷魚

羅爾德·達爾 *Roald Dahl* ◎著

昆丁·布雷克 *Quentin Blake* ◎繪

顏銘新◎譯

The Enormous Crocodile

振聲高中
張湘君 校長 強力推薦

開啟孩子創造力
由閱讀羅爾德・達爾開始

張湘君（振聲高中校長）

　　羅爾德・達爾（1916—1990）是一位備受矚目的英國兒童文學大師級人物。他的十九部作品，部部想像力驚人，書中創意點子令人拍案叫絕，受到廣大小讀者的喜愛，甚至還有個羅爾德・達爾日（9月13日），當天全球粉絲們紛紛舉辦各種活動，向羅爾德・達爾這位偉大的作者致敬。

　　我個人是達爾迷，他的作品不管是各種版本的作品、錄音帶或錄影帶甚至考題，我都廣泛蒐集。在國立臺北教育大學兒童英語教育研究所及亞洲大學應用外語學系教授「英美兒童文學」期間，更是將達爾的作品列入學生修課必讀書單，也不時在課堂中播放其作品改拍的電影《飛天巨桃歷險記》、《巧克力工廠的祕密》、《吹夢巨人》、《小魔女》及《女巫》，以增加學生對達爾作品不同面向的探索及體悟。

　　達爾創作之兒童讀物所以受人矚目，除了寫作手法高明

外，主要是因為其大量運用獨特的「殘酷式幽默」，令學校老師不安，孩子的家長不悅，評論家不屑。達爾常在作品中敘述種種殘忍的場面或手段，例如把人斬成肉泥、絞成肉醬、搗爛他、砸碎他等等，這些事看在小孩子的眼裡，是有趣、誇張、惹人捧腹大笑，然而看在大人眼裡，盡是血腥恐怖、殘忍不堪，一文不值。

　　例如，《神奇魔指》書中描述一個小女孩的指頭有神奇的魔力，當她氣憤、失去控制的時候，全身會先變得很熱、很熱，右手的指尖也會開始產生帶著奔馳閃光的電流，而這電流會跳出去觸擊令她氣憤的人，他們的身上就會接二連三的發生怪事。達爾運用了「殘酷式幽默」來傳達孩子愛護動物的心聲，誇張、有趣、三不五時帶點殘忍場面的情節，非常能吸引小讀者閱讀。

達爾有四個孩子，每天晚上他在孩子睡覺前，也都會說故事給他們聽，因此，他的魅力不只是在文字，擅長用聲音來說故事應該也算是他的另一項特異功能。達爾常自己造字，來增加口說故事時的生動。以《大大大大的鱷魚》為例，書中有許多英文動詞鮮活傳神，如 squish、squizzle、swizzle、swoosh、Trunky 等一般字典裡查不到的「達爾專用字」，讀者可仔細推敲這些字的來源，或輕鬆略過，但不要忘了享受其中的音韻樂趣。尤其對白鮮活有趣的英文章節，可鼓勵小讀者從事英語話劇或讀者劇場的演出。

達爾是個喜歡搞怪的人，他搞怪的能力無遠弗屆，尤其擅長創造魔法的情節和運用幻想的元素，這可能跟達爾的母親在他和他的姊妹們孩提時代，常常說巨人等虛構人物的北歐神話故事有關。然而達爾對自己的作品要求嚴格，絕不重複使用相同的點子，往往一年才能醞釀出一個滿意的故事。

總之，達爾是那種只想要給孩子快樂的作家，他的作品中，

孩子是絕對的王，孩子的對手（通常是大人）通常都會得到嚴厲不留情的懲罰。這些過程驚悚的反大人作品，如同《小鬼當家》一系列的電影，披露小孩其實擁有遇事沉著、冷靜、聰明、機智應對的大能力，著實讓大人驚訝！而小讀者閱讀達爾作品後，應該也能學到不管遇到多大困難，都要鎮定自若，勇敢面對，更要積極的想辦法，用自己的智慧和經驗去戰勝它！

　　紅花要有綠葉襯，三本書的插畫皆由昆丁・布萊克執筆，相得益彰。昆丁・布萊克是當代英國兒童文學界最負盛名的插畫家和作家，得過英國兒童讀物的各項大獎，他風格滑稽特異的插畫與達爾的精闢文字可謂天生一對，是無可取代的組合。

　　近年來，世界上有為的政府莫不以打造創造力國度為施政主軸，希望國家百姓能具備自我創造的意識，勇於創新、冒險與超越，以開闊的思維和自在的態度展現獨特、新奇和有趣之個人色彩，並從不斷嘗試創造的過程中發現學習樂趣。

　　達爾作品總能帶給讀者豐富的想像力、創造力及閱讀的樂趣，在此我誠摯的、歡喜的將它的新版推薦給臺灣的大小讀者。

謹將本書獻給蘇菲

羅爾德・達爾

大大大大**的鱷魚**

在非洲最寬大、最汙褐、最泥濘的河流裡，有

兩隻鱷魚把頭稍稍抬出水面優閒的躺著。其中一隻

體型超級無敵的大（我們稱牠為**大大大大鱷魚**）。

另一隻雖然體型還滿大，但就沒有那麼大。

　　「你曉得我今天午餐要吃什麼嗎？」大大大大

鱷魚問。

　　「不曉得，」還滿大鱷魚說：「你要吃什麼？」

　　大大大大鱷魚露出上百顆尖銳的白色牙齒，不

懷好意的獰笑著，「今天的午餐，」牠說：「我想

吃一個香甜多汁的小孩。」

「我從來不吃小孩，」還滿大鱷魚說：「我只吃魚。」

「ㄏㄡ！ㄏㄡ！ㄏㄡ！」大大大大鱷魚大叫道：「我敢打賭，假如這個時候，你瞧見了一個胖嘟嘟、甜滋滋的小孩在那裡玩水，你會咕嚕一口吞下他！」

「不，我才不會！」還滿大鱷魚說：「孩子太硬太難咬了。不僅又硬又難咬，而且味道還很噁很苦。」

「**又硬又難咬？**」大大大大鱷魚大叫道：「**很噁很苦？**聽你在胡扯！他們是汁多味美！」

「小孩嘗起來很苦，」還滿大鱷魚說：「在吃之前，還得用糖把他們全身塗滿才吃得下去。」

　　「小孩比魚還要大，」大大大大鱷魚說：「可以享受到更豐盛的一餐。」

　　「你好貪心哦，」還滿大鱷魚說：「你是整條河裡最貪心的鱷仔。」

「我是整條河裡最勇敢的鱷仔，」大大大大鱷魚說：「我是唯一敢離開水裡、穿越森林、進到鎮上去找小孩來吃的鱷魚。」

「你才去過一次而已，」還滿大鱷魚帶著鄙視語氣說：「結果咧？你不但被看到了，而且還逃之夭夭。」

「啊，不過我今天去的話，他們無論如何都看不到我。」大大大大鱷魚說。

「他們當然看得到你，」還滿大鱷魚說：「你的體形是那麼宇宙超級無敵的龐大，長相又這麼醜陋，他們在好幾哩外就會看見你了。」

大大大大鱷魚又狡猾的笑了起來，牠那滿口嚇人的尖銳牙齒在陽光下像刀子一樣的閃爍著。「不會有人看見我的，」牠說：「因為這一次，我已經想好一套祕密計畫和聰明計謀。」

「**聰明計謀？**」還滿大鱷魚叫道：「你這輩子可從來沒做過一件聰明事！你是整條河裡最愚笨的鱷仔了！」

「我是整條河裡最聰明的鱷仔。」大大大大鱷

魚回答道：「在你躺在河裡挨餓的時候，肥嫩多汁

的小孩可是讓我今天午餐的時候，能夠好好的大快朵頤一番。再見！」

　　說完，大大大大鱷魚便游到岸邊，並且爬出了水面。

河岸上滑滑黏黏的爛泥裡，正好有一隻龐然大物站在那兒。那是河馬俏翹臀。

「哈囉，哈囉，」俏翹臀說：「大白天的這種時候，你究竟打算上哪兒去啊？」

「我現在有一套祕密計畫和聰明計謀。」鱷魚說。

「我的天，」俏翹臀說：「我敢打賭，你一定是想去做些令人討厭的事。」

大大大大鱷魚對著俏翹臀猙獰的笑說：

「現在我要出發去，

找個美味的東西，

來塞滿我飢腸轆轆的肚皮，

好吃、好吃，美味至極！」

「什麼東西這麼好吃？」俏翹臀問。

「你猜猜看，」大大大大鱷魚說：「那是用兩條腿走路的一種東西。」

「該不會是……」俏翹臀說：「你的**意思**該不會是說你要去吃小孩子吧？」

「當然是囉！」鱷魚說。

「噢，你這隻可怕的、貪心的、殘暴的野獸！」俏翹臀大叫：「我希望你被抓去煮成鱷魚湯！」

大大大大鱷魚對著俏翹臀放聲大笑。接著牠便一晃離開進到森林裡去了。

進到森林裡後，大大大大鱷魚碰到了大象壯壯鼻。壯壯鼻正一口一口的慢慢吃著高高樹梢上的葉子，一開始並沒有注意到鱷魚。所以鱷魚在大象的腿上咬了一口。

　　「哇！」壯壯鼻用低沉宏亮的聲音說：「誰咬我？哦，是你。你這野蠻無禮的鱷魚！你怎麼不滾回去屬於你那汙褐泥濘的大河裡？」

　　「我現在有一套祕密計畫和聰明計謀呢！」鱷魚說。

　　「你是說，你有**討人厭**的計畫和**惹人厭**的詭計嗎？」壯壯鼻說：「你這輩子根本沒做過一件好事！」

大大大大鱷魚仰著臉看著壯壯鼻，不懷好意的

咧嘴笑說：

「鮮嫩多汁的小孩，

我去找來當午餐啦！

接著，你聽見了嗎？

他的骨頭嘎啦嘎啦！」

「噢，你這邪惡野蠻的野獸！」壯壯鼻大叫：「噢，你這粗鄙噁心的惡魔！我希望你被壓扁！被碾碎！還有被攪得爛爛的煮成燉鱷魚！」

大大大大鱷魚大聲狂笑，並且走進濃密的森林裡消失了。

　　走沒多遠，鱷魚碰到了猴子麻果昂波。麻果昂
波正坐在樹上吃著堅果。

　　「哈囉，阿鱷，」麻果昂波說：「你這個時候
來這兒做啥？」

　　「我有一套祕密計畫和聰明計謀咧！」鱷魚說。

「想要來點堅果吃吃嗎？」麻果昂波問。

「我有比堅果更好的東西可以吃。」鱷魚語帶不屑的說。

「我認為**再也沒有**比堅果更好吃的東西了。」麻果昂波說。

「啊──哈！」大大大大鱷魚說：

「我所要吃的這種東西，

身上不但有指頭、腳趾甲和手臂，

腿和腳還可以當點心！」

麻果昂波臉色發白，開始全身顫抖。「你該不

會真的要去吞食小孩子吧，不會吧？」牠說。

「當然是真的！」鱷魚說：「連衣服一起吃。

他們連衣服一起吃，品嘗起來更美味。」

「噢，你這可怕的、貪吃的鱷仔！」麻果昂波

大叫：「你這狡猾的畜牲！我希望鈕釦、帶釦全部
卡住你的喉嚨，把你噎死！」

　　大大大大鱷魚仰著頭對麻果昂波猙獰的笑說：
「我也吃猴子。」接著牠把自己的巨顎一張，快得

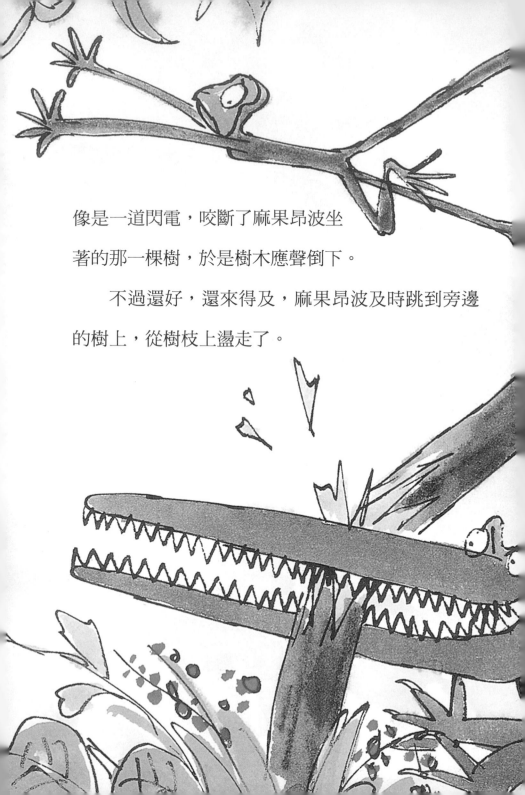

像是一道閃電，咬斷了麻果昂波坐

著的那一棵樹，於是樹木應聲倒下。

　　不過還好，還來得及，麻果昂波及時跳到旁邊

的樹上，從樹枝上盪走了。

再走沒多遠，大大大大鱷魚碰到了布丁捲鳥，布丁捲鳥正在橘子樹上築巢。

「哈囉你好，大大大大鱷魚！」布丁捲鳥唱著：「我們挺少在這森林裡看到你。」

「啊，」鱷魚說：「因為我腦袋裡有一套祕密計畫和聰明計謀！」

「希望不是些討人厭的事情。」布丁捲鳥唱著。

「**什麼討人厭！**」鱷魚大叫：「當然不會討人厭！是很可口！」

「它氣味誘人，它超級可口，

它軟軟糊糊，它美味多多，

它的味道賽過酸腐陳年魚。

你搗糊它，你嚼爛它！

你啃光它，你壓扁它！

聽到它嘎吱碎窣的聲音是多麼的悅耳！」

「那一定是莓子，」布丁捲鳥唱著：「莓子是全世界我最愛的食物。也許那是覆盆子？或可能是草莓？」

大大大大鱷魚笑得很厲害，笑到自己的牙齒就像撲滿裡的硬幣一樣鏗鏘作響，「鱷魚不吃莓子的，」牠說：「我們吃小男生和小女生，而且有時候我們也吃布丁捲鳥。」說時遲、那時快，鱷魚抬起下顎對準布丁捲鳥猛地咬去，差一點就咬住鳥兒了。不過牠還是使勁兒咬到鳥兒尾巴上漂亮的長羽毛。布丁捲鳥慌張的尖叫一聲，馬上筆直衝上天空，留下了尾羽在大大大大鱷魚的嘴巴裡。

　　終於，大大大大鱷魚從茂密森林的另一端走出來，見到了陽光，牠可以看見不遠處的小鎮。

　　「ㄏㄡ、ㄏㄡ！」牠大聲的自言自語說著：「哈、哈！剛剛經過森林那一段路，讓我比剛剛更餓了。

今天一個小孩子幾乎不夠我吃。若沒吃掉三個味美

多汁的小孩，我是不可能會吃飽的！」

　　於是，牠開始爬向鎮上去。

大大大大鱷魚爬到一個滿是椰子樹的地方。

牠知道鎮上的孩子經常來這裡找椰子。這些樹對他們來說太高了，沒法兒爬上去，但在地上總會有些掉下來的椰子。

大大大大鱷魚動作俐落的把掉在地上的椰子全收集起來，並撿了幾枝掉下來的樹枝。

「現在開始進行聰明計謀第一招！」牠低聲對著自己說：「很快就可以吃到我的第一份午餐了。」

首先，牠把全部的椰子樹枝放在牠的牙齒間咬著。

前爪抓著椰子，然後用尾巴把自己豎立起來，好平衡在半空中直挺挺的身子。

牠絞盡腦汁擺好樹枝和椰子，讓自己看起來就像豎立在大椰子樹叢中的一棵小椰子樹。

　　不一會兒，兩個小孩走了過來。他們是兄妹。男孩叫作托托，妹妹叫作瑪麗。他們邊走邊尋找掉下來的椰子，但是根本就找不到，因為大大大大鱷魚已經全拿光了。

　　「噢，看！」托托叫：「那裡那棵樹比其他樹

矮多了！而且長
滿了椰子！我想，
開始爬上去的那
一段，如果妳先幫我
一下，我應該可以很
容易爬上那棵樹。」

　　於是，托托和瑪麗朝著他們誤
認的那棵小椰子樹跑過去。

　　大大大大鱷魚從樹枝中偷瞄出
去，看見他們愈走愈近。牠舔了
舔嘴唇，開始興奮
得流著口水。

突然間傳來了一陣驚人的咻轟巨響。是河馬俏翹臀。牠噴著粗重的鼻息從森林中猛力衝出來，低著頭疾速奔馳。

「托托，小心！」俏翹臀吼叫：「瑪麗，小心！那不是椰子樹！那是大大大大鱷魚，牠想把你們吃光光！」

俏翹臀正面撞擊大大大大鱷魚。

俏翹臀的巨大腦袋擊中了鱷魚，立刻將牠撞飛出去。

「哦——咦！」鱷魚大叫：「救命啊！停下來！我現在在哪兒？」

托托和瑪麗用最快的速度逃回鎮上。

不過鱷魚是很強壯結實的，即使是河馬也很難傷害到牠。

大大大大鱷魚自己站了起來，爬向兒童遊樂場。

「現在進行聰明計謀第二招！」牠告訴自己：「這招一定管用！」

那時候並沒有任何小孩在遊樂場裡頭玩。他們都在上課。

大大大大鱷魚找來了一大塊木頭，放在遊樂場正中間。然後牠趴在那塊木頭上，把腳全都縮攏起來，好讓自己看起來完全就像是一具翹翹板。

放學後，孩子們全部都奔向了遊樂場。

「噢，看！」他們大叫：「我們有新的翹翹板耶！」

他們全部擠了過來，興奮的叫喊著。

「好耶！我先上去！」

「我坐另一邊去！」

「我要先去！」

「我也要！我也要！」

然後，有一個比其他小孩年紀稍大的女孩說：

「這真是個滿布疙瘩的奇怪翹翹板，不是嗎？你們

覺得坐上去安全嗎？」

46

「當然安全！」其他孩子說：「它看起來堅固得跟什麼似的！」

大大大大鱷魚瞇開一隻眼睛瞄著擠在他周圍的孩子們，心想，很快的，其中一個小孩就會坐到我的頭上，接著我只要猛力一扭、喀滋一口，然後接著就是**好吃好吃好吃**。

就在此時，閃現了一抹棕色身影，有個東西跳進了遊樂場中間，蹦到了鞦韆上。

是猴子麻果昂波。

「快逃！」麻果昂波對著孩子大喊。

「你們大夥兒，逃，逃，逃！那不是翹翹板！那是大大大大鱷魚，而且牠打算把你們吃光光！」

孩子們尖叫著逃命。

然後，麻果昂波跑回森林裡消失了，只剩大大大大鱷魚獨自留在遊樂場中。

大大大大的鱷魚

鱷魚咒罵著猴子，蹣跚的晃回草叢中躲了起來。

「我愈來愈餓了！」牠自言自語的說：「現在至少要四個小孩，我才吃得飽！」

大大大大鱷魚在小鎮邊上爬行，小心著避免被瞧見。

牠來到一個準備舉行慶典活動的地方，那裡有溜滑梯和盪秋千和碰碰車，還有賣爆米花和棉花糖

的人。那裡還有一座很大的旋轉木馬。

旋轉木馬上有做得唯妙唯肖、可以讓小朋友騎在上面的木頭動物，有白馬和獅子和老虎和長了魚尾巴的美人魚，還有嘴裡吐出紅色舌頭的可怕的龍。

「現在進行聰明計謀第三招。」大大大大鱷魚舔舔嘴脣說。

趁沒人看到的時候，牠爬上了旋轉木馬，把自己安置在木頭獅子和可怕的龍中間。牠用自己的兩條後腿半坐半站著，保持靜止不動，看起來完全就像是一隻在旋轉木馬上的木頭鱷魚。

不一會兒，所有的小孩蜂擁而進這個舉行節慶的場地，有些孩

子跑向旋轉木馬，顯得非常興奮。

「我要去騎龍！」一個叫道。

「我要去坐可愛的白馬！」另一個叫。

「我要去騎獅子！」第三個叫。

接著有一個叫吉兒的小女孩說：「我要去騎那一隻好笑的老木頭鱷魚！」

大大大大鱷魚還是保持靜止不動，但是看得到朝牠跑過來的小女孩。

「好吃──好吃──好好吃，」牠想：「我可以輕輕鬆鬆的咕嚕一口就吞下她了。」

突然之間一陣**咻咻**一陣**颼颼**，有個東西從空中咻咻颼颼的出現了。

52

那是布丁捲鳥。

牠在旋轉木馬的周圍盤旋又盤旋的飛著，唱出：「小心，吉兒！小心！小心！別騎上那隻鱷魚！」

吉兒停下來往天空看。

「那不是木頭鱷魚！」布丁捲鳥唱著：「那是真正的鱷魚！牠是從河裡來的大大大大鱷魚，而且牠打算吃掉妳！」

吉兒轉身就逃，其他小孩也是，連在旋轉木馬中工作的人也跳出旋轉木馬，用盡全力的逃跑。

大大大大鱷魚咒罵了布丁捲鳥幾聲，最後只能蹣跚的晃回草叢中躲起來。

「我現在餓得前胸貼後背，」牠對著自己說：
「我得吃六個小孩才會飽！」

　　就在小鎮外，有一小片被樹叢和灌木叢圍著的
美麗小空地。這裡是野餐區。那兒有不少木頭桌子
和長板凳，好讓人們隨時都可以去那
兒野餐。

大大大大鱷魚爬到了野餐區。那裡空無一人。

「現在進行聰明計謀第四招！」牠悄聲對自己說。

牠撿了一束可愛的花朵，並且把花布置在其中一張桌子上。

再從同一張桌子旁邊移走了一條板凳，把那條

板凳藏在灌木叢裡。然後把自己放在剛剛那條板凳
原來擺放的地方。

　　牠把自己的頭縮攏在胸部下方，把尾巴捲藏起
來，把自己偽裝成一條有四隻腳的木頭長板凳。

　　沒多久，有兩個男孩和兩個女孩帶著幾籃食物
走過來了。他們是一家人，他們的媽媽告訴他們可

以出來一起野餐。

「我們要坐在哪
張桌子呢?」其中一個
說。

「那我們選那一張上面有可愛花朵的桌子。」
另一個說。

大大大大鱷魚安靜得像隻老鼠。「我要把他們
全部吃掉,」牠自言自語:「他們就快坐到我背上
來了,接著我只要快速的甩一甩我的頭,再
來就可以**嘎吱碎窣咕嚕**!」

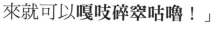

突然間一個宏亮低沉的聲音從森林裡傳出來：
「退回去，孩子們！退回去！退回去！」

　　孩子們停了下來，朝著聲音傳來的方向望了
過去。接著，看到大象壯壯鼻撞開樹枝，飛奔出
森林。

「你們可不要坐上那條板凳！」壯壯鼻怒吼著：「牠是大大大大鱷魚，而且牠打算把你們全部吃光光！」

壯壯鼻衝到了大大大大鱷魚所在的位置，牠的象鼻子快如閃電一般，瞬間就捲住鱷魚尾巴，把鱷魚吊在半空中。

「嘿！放我走！」大大大大鱷魚頭尾顛倒被倒吊著，牠大叫：「放我走！放我走！」

「不，」 壯壯鼻說：「我不放你走。我們都受夠了你口中的聰明計謀。」

壯壯鼻開始在半空中一圈又一圈的轉著鱷魚。

一開始慢慢的轉著。

然後稍微轉得快一點……

然後再快一點……

然後更快……

然後

再快、再快……

再更快……

很快的，

大大大大鱷魚變成

壯壯鼻腦袋周圍的

一團模糊影子。

突然間，壯壯鼻放掉了鱷魚的尾巴，接著鱷魚有如一艘巨大的綠色火箭般衝入雲霄。

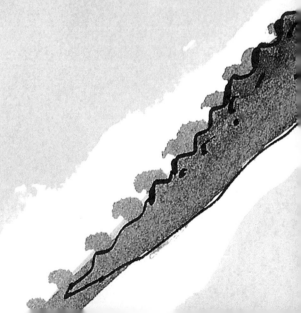

愈來愈高、愈來愈高……

更高……

還要

更高……

更快……

然後

又更快……

牠飛得那麼的快、那麼的高，所以，才一下子，地球變成數哩之遙的一個小黑點了。

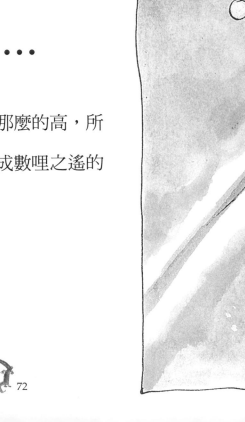

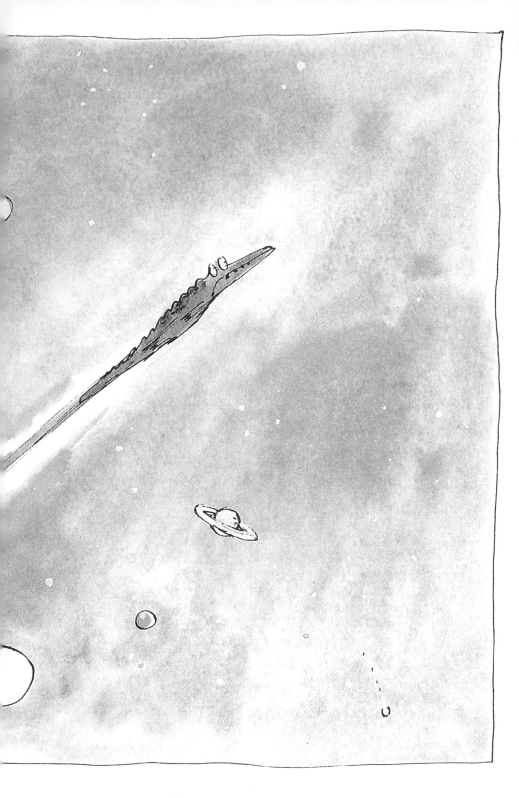

咻──牠繼續高飛、再高飛……

咻──遠遠的飛進太空中……

咻──飛過月球……

咻──飛過恆星和行星……

直到最後……

伴隨著最威力無窮的一聲

砰！

接著大大大大鱷魚一頭栽進了熱得
滾燙的太陽。

然後就像條香腸一樣，「嘶──」
一聲就被烤熟了！

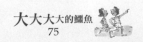

TO Sophie

R.D.

ROALD DAHL
The Enormous Crocodile

In the biggest, brownest muddiest river in Africa,

two crocodiles lay with their heads just above the water.

One of the crocodiles was enormous. The other was not so big.

"Do you know what I would like for my lunch today?" the Enormous Crocodile[1] asked.

"No," the Notsobig One[2] said. "What?"

The Enormous Crocodile grinned, showing hundreds of sharp white teeth. "For my lunch today," he said, "I would like a nice juicy little child."

"I never eat children," the Notsobig One said. "Only fish."

"Ho, ho, ho!" cried the Enormous Crocodile. "I'll bet if you saw a fat juicy little child paddling in the water over there at this very moment, you'd gulp him up in one gollop**3** !"

"No, I wouldn't," the Notsobig One said.

"Children are too tough and chewy. They are tough and chewy and nasty and bitter."

"Tough and chewy!" cried the Enormous Crocodile. *"Nasty and bitter!* What awful tommy-rot**4** you talk! They are juicy and yummy!"

"They taste so bitter," the Notsobig One said, "you have to cover them with sugar before you can eat them."

"Children are bigger than fish,"said the Enormous Crocodile. "You get bigger helpings."

"You are greedy," the Notsobig One said. "You're the greediest croc in the whole river."

"I'm the bravest croc in the whole river," said the Enormous Crocodile. "I'm the only one who dares to leave the water and go through the jungle to the town to look for little children to eat."

"You've only done that once," snorted the Notsobig One. "And what happened then? They all saw you coming and ran away."

"Ah, but today when I go, they won't see me at all," said the Enormous Crocodile.

"Of course they'll see you," the Notsobig One said. "You're so enormous and ugly, they'll see you from miles away."

The Enormous Crocodile grinned again, and his terrible sharp teeth sparkled like knives in the sun. "Nobody will see me," he said, "because this time I've thought up secret plans and clever tricks."

"*Clever tricks?*" cried the Notsobig One. "You've never done anything clever in your life! You're the stupidest croc on the whole river!"

"I'm the cleverest croc on the whold river," the

Enormous Crocodile answered. "For my lunch today I

shall feast upon a fat juicy little child while you lie here in the river feeling hungry. Goodbye."

The Enormous Crcodile swam to the side of the river, and crawled out of the water.

A gigantic creature was standing in the slimy oozy mud on the river-bank. It was Humpy-Rumpy[5], the Hippopotamus.

"Hello, hello," said Humpy-Rumpy. "Where on earth[6] are you off to at this time of day?"

"I have secret plans and clever tricks," said the Crocodile.

"Oh dear," said Humpy-Rumpy. "I'll bet you're going to do something horrid."

The Enormous Crocodile grinned at Humpy-Rumpy and said:

"I'm going to fill my

hungry empty tummy

With something yummy

yummy yummy yummy!"

"What's so yummy?" asked Humpy-Rumpy.

"Try to guess," said the Crocodile. "It's something that walks on two legs."

"You don't mean … " said Humpy-Rumpy. "You don't *really* mean you're going to eat a little child?"

"Of course I am," said the Crocodile.

"Oh, you horrid greedy grumptious[7] brute!" cried Humpy-Rumpy. "I hope you get caught and cooked and turned into crocodile soup!"

The Enormous Crocodile laughed out loud at Humpy-Rumpy. Then he waddled[8] off into the jungle.

Inside the jungle, he met Trunky[9], the Elephant. Trunky was nibbling leaves from the top of a tall tree, and he didn't notice the Crocodile at first. So the Crocodile bit him on the leg.

"Ow!" said Trunky in his big deep voice. "Who did that? Oh, it's you, is it, you beastly Crocodile. Why don't you go back to the big brown muddy river where you belong?"

"I have secret plans and clever tricks," said the Crocodile.

"You mean you've *nasty* plans and *nasty* tricks," said Trunky. "You've never done a nice thing in your life."

The Enormous Crocodile grinned up at Trunky and said:

"I'm off to find a yummy

child for lunch.

Keep listening and you'll hear

the bones go crunch!"

"Oh, you wicked beastly beast!" cried Trunky. "Oh, you foul[10] and filthy[11] fiend[12] ! I hope you get squashed[13] and squished[14] and squizzled[15] and boiled up into crocodile stew!"

The Enormous Crocodile laughed out loud and disappeared into the thick jungle.

A bit further on, he met Muggle-Wump[16] , the Monkey. Muggle-Wump was sitting in a tree, eating nuts.

"Hello, Crocky," said Muggle-Wump. "What are you up to now?"

"I have secret plans and clever tricks," said the Crocodile.

"Would you like some nuts?" askd Muggle-Wump.

"I have better things to eat than nuts," sniffed the Crocodile.

"I didn't think there was anything better than nuts," said Muggle-Wump.

"Ah-ha," said the Enormous Crocodile,

"The sort of things that

I'm going to eat

have fingers, toe-nails, arms

and legs and feet!"

Muggle-Wump went pale and began to shake all over. "You aren't really going to gobble up a little child, are you?" he said.

"Of course I am," said the Crocodile. "Clothes and all. They taste better with the clothes on."

"Oh, you horrid hoggish[17] croc!" cried Muggle-Wump. "You slimy creature! I hope the buttons and buckles all stick in your throat and choke you to death!"

The Crocodile grinned up at Muggle-Wump and said, "I eat monkeys, too." And quick as a flash, with

one bite of his huge jaws, he bit

through the tree that Muggle-Wump

was sitting in, and down it came.

But just in time, Muggle-Wump jumped

into the next tree and swung away

through the branches.

A bit further on, the Enormous Crocodile met the Roly-Poly[18] Bird. The Roly-Poly Bird was building a nest in an orange tree.

"Hello there, Enormous Crocodile!" sang the Roly-Poly Bird. "We don't often see you up here in the jungle."

"Ah," said the Crocodile. "I have secret plans and clever tricks."

"I hope it's not something nasty." sang the Roly-Poly Bird.

"*Nasty!*" cried the Crocodile. "Of course it's not nasty! It's delicious!"

"It's luscious[19], it's super,

It's mushious[20], it's duper[21],

It's better than rotten old fish.

You mash[22] it and munch[23] it,

You chew it and crunch[24] it!

It's lovely to hear it go squish[25]!"

"It must be berries," sang the Roly-Poly Bird. "Berries are my favourite food in the world. Is it raspberries, perhaps? Or could it be strawberries?"

The Enormous Crocodile laughed so much his teeth rattled together like pennies in a moneybox. "Crocodiles don't eat berries," he said. "We eat little boys and girls. And sometimes we eat Roly-Poly Birds, as well." Very

quickly, the Crocodile reached up and snapped his jaws at the Roly-Poly Bird. He just missed the Bird, but he managed to catch hold of the long beautiful feathers in its tail. The Roly-Poly Bird gave a shriek of terror and shot straight up into the air, leaving its tail feathers behind in the Enormous Crocodile's mouth.

At last, the Enormous Crocodile came out of the other side of the jungle into the sunshine. He could see the town not far away.

"Ho-ho!" he said, talking aloud to himself. "Ha-ha! That walk through the jungle has made me hungrier than ever. One child isn't going to be nearly enough for me today. I won't be full up until I've eaten at least three juicy little children!"

He started to creep forward towards the town.

The Enormous Crocodile crept over to a place where there were a lot of coconut trees.

He knew that children from the town often came here looking for coconuts. The trees were too tall for them to climb, but there were always some coconuts on the ground that had fallen down.

The Enormous Crocodile quickly collected all the coconuts that were lying on the ground. He also gathered together several fallen branches.

"Now for Clever Trick Number One!" he whispered to himself. "It won't be long before I am eating the first part of my lunch!"

He took all the coconut branches and held them between his teeth.

He grasped the coconuts in his front paws. Then he stood straight up in the air, balancing himself on his tail.

He arranged the branches and the coconuts so cleverly that he now looked exactly like a small coconut

tree standing among the big coconut
trees.

Soon, two children came
along. They were brother
and sister. The boy
was called Toto. His
sister was called Mary.
They walked around
looking for fallen coconuts,
but they couldn't find any because the
Enormous Crocodile had gathered them all
up.

"Oh look!"cried Toto. "That tree over there is much smaller than the others! And it's full of coconuts! I think I could climb that one quite easily if you help me up the first bit."

Toto and Mary ran towards what they thought was the small coconut tree.

The Enormous Crocodile peered through the

branches, watching them
as they came closer
and closer. He licked
his lips. He began to
dribble with excitement.

Suddenly there was
a tremendous whooshing[26]
noise. It was Humpy-Rumpy, the
Hippopotamus. He came crashing and
snorting out of the jungle. His head was
down low and he was galloping[27] at a
terrific speed.

"Look out, Toto!" shouted Humpy-Rumpy. "Look

out, Mary! That's not a coconut tree! It's the Enormous

Crocodile and he wants to eat you up!"

Humpy-Rumpy charged

straight at the Enormous

Crocodile. He caught

him with his giant head and sent him tumbling[28] and skidding[29] over the ground.

"Ow-eeee!" cried the Crocodile. "Help! Stop! Where am I?"

Toto and Mary ran back to the town as fast as they could.

But crocodiles are tough. It is difficult for even a hippopotamus to hurt them.

The Enormous Crocodile picked himself up and crept towards the place where the children's playground was.

"Now for Clever Trick Number Two!"he said to

himself. "This one is certain to work!"

There were no children in the playground at that moment. They were all in school.

The Enormous Crocodile found a large piece of wood and placed it in the middle of the playground. Then he lay across the piece of wood and tucked in his feet so that he looked almost exactly like a see-saw.

When school was over, the children all came running on to the playground.

"Oh look!" they cried. "We've got a new see-saw!"

They all crowded round, shouting with excitement.

"Bags[30] I have the first go!"

"I'll get on the other end!"

"I want to go first!"

"So do I! So do I!"

Then, a girl who was older than the others said, "It's rather a funny knobbly[31] sort of a see-saw, isn't it? Do you think it'll be safe to sit on?"

"Of course it will!" the others said. "It looks

strong as anything!"

The Enormous Crocodile opened one eye just a tiny bit and watched the children who were crowding around him. Soon, he thought, one of them is going to sit on my head, then I will give a jerk and a snap, and after that it will be *yum yum yum*.

At that moment, there was a flash of brown and something jumped into the playground and hopped up on to the top of the swings.

It was Muggle-Wump, the Monkey.

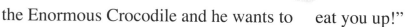

"Run!" Muggle-Wump shouted to the children. "All of you, run, run, run! That's not a see-saw! It's the Enormous Crocodile and he wants to eat you up!"

The children screamed and ran for their lives.

Muggle-Wump disappeared back into the jungle, and the Enormous Crocodile was left all alone in the playground.

He cursed the Monkey and waddled back into the bushes to hide.

"I'm getting hungrier and hungrier!" he said. "I shall have to eat at least four children now before I am full up!"

The Enormous Crocodile crept around the edge of the town, taking great care not to be seen.

He came to a place where they were getting ready to have a fair. There were slides and swings and dodgem-cars[32] and people selling popcorn and candy-floss[33]. There was also a big roundabout[34].

The roundabout had marvellous wooden creatures for the children to ride on. There were white horses and lions and tigers and mermaids with fishes' tails and fearsome dragons with red tongues sticking out of their mouths.

"Now for Clever Trick Number Three," said the Enormous Crocodile, licking his lips.

When no one was looking, he crept up on to the roundabout

and put himself between a wooden lion and a fearsome dragon. He sat up a bit on his back legs and he kept very still. He looked exactly like a wooden crocodile on the roundabout.

Soon, all sorts of children came flocking[35] into the fair. Several of them ran towards the roundabout. They were very excited.

"I'm going to ride on a dragon!" cried one.

"I'm going on a lovely white horse!" cried another.

"I'm going on a lion!" cried a third one.

And one little girl, whose name was Jill said, "*I'm going to ride on that funny old wooden crocodile!*"

The Enormous Crocodile kept very still, but he could see the little girl coming towards him. "Yummy-yum-yum," he thought. "I'll gulp her up easily in one gollop."

Suddenly there was a swish³⁶ and a *swoosh*³⁷ and something came swishing and swooshing out of the sky.

It was the Roly-Poly Bird.

He flew round and round the roundabout, singing, "Look out, Jill! Look out. Look out. Don't ride on that crocodile!"

Jill stopped and looked up.

"That's not a wooden crocodile!" sang the Roly-Poly Bird. "It's a real one! It's the Enormous Crocodile from the river and he wants to eat you up!"

Jill turned and ran. So did all the other children. Even the man who was working the roundabout jumped off it and ran away as fast as he could.

The Enormous Crocodile cursed the Roly-Poly Bird and waddled back into the bushes to hide.

"I'm so hungry now," he said to himself, "I could eat six children before I am full up!"

Just outside the town, there was a pretty little field with trees and bushes all round it. This was called The

Picnic Place. There were several wooden tables and long benches, and people were allowed to go there and have a picnic at any time.

The Enormous Crocodile crept over to The Picnic Place. There was no one in sight.

"Now for Clever Trick Number Four!" he whispered to himself.

He picked a lovely bunch of flowers and arranged it

on one of the tables.

From the same table, he took away one of the

benches and hid it in the bushes.Then he put himself in

the place where the bench had been.

By tucking his head under his chest, and by twisting

his tail out of sight, he made himself look very much

like a long wooden bench with four legs.

Soon, two boys and two girls came along carrying

baskets of food. They were all from one family, and their mother had said they could go out and have a picnic together.

"Which table shall we sit at?" said one.

"Let's take the table with the lovely flowers on it," said another.

The Enormous Crocodile kept as quiet as a mouse. "I shall eat them all," he said to himself. "They will come and sit on my back and I will swizzle**38** my head around quickly, and after that it'll be *squish crunch gollop*."

Suddenly a big deep voice from the jungle shouted, "Stand back, children! Stand back! Stand back!"

The children stopped and stared at the place where the voice was coming from.

Then, with a crashing of branches, Trunky the Elephant came rushing out of the jungle.

"That's not a bench you were going to sit on!" he

bellowed. "It's the Enormous Crocodile, and he wants to

eat you all up!"

Trunky trotted over to the spot where the Enormous Crocodile was standing, and quick as a flash he wrapped his trunk around the Crocodile's tail and hoisted him up into the air.

"Hey! Let me go!" yelled the Enormous Crocodile, who was now dangling upside down. "Let me go! Let me go!"

"No," Trunky said. "I will not let you go. We've all had quite enough of your clever tricks."

Trunky began to swing the Crocodile round and round in the air. At first he swung him slowly.

Then he swung him faster …

And FASTER...
And FASTER...

And
FASTER
STILL...

Soon the

Enormous

Crocodile was

just a blurry

circle going

round and round

Trunky's head.

Suddenly, Trunky let go of
the Crocodile's tail, and the
Crocodile went shooting
high up into the sky like
a huge green rocket.

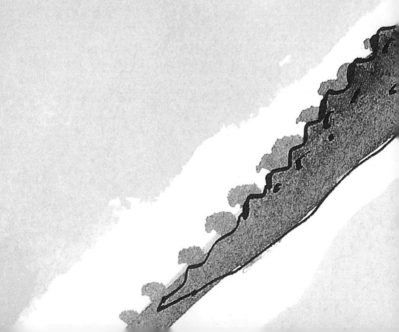

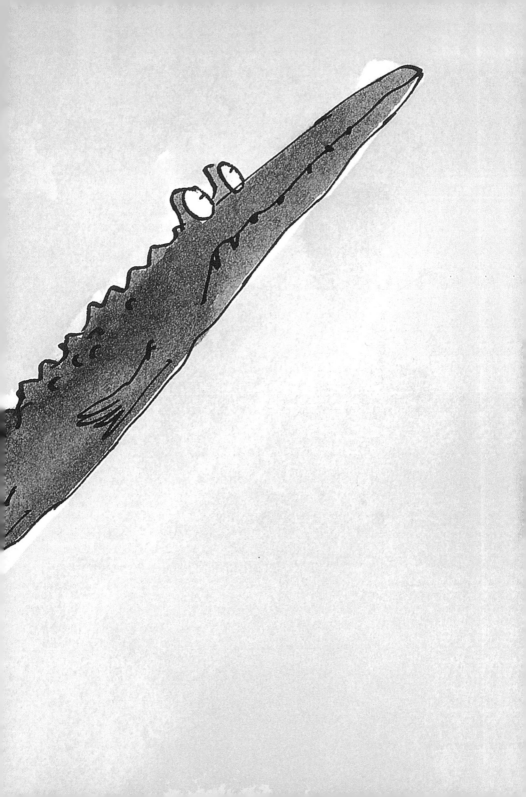

Up and up he went ...

HIGHER

and

HIGHER ...
FASTER

and

FASTER ...

He was going so fast and so
high that soon the earth was just a
tiny dot miles below.

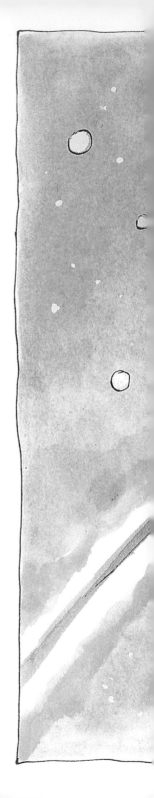

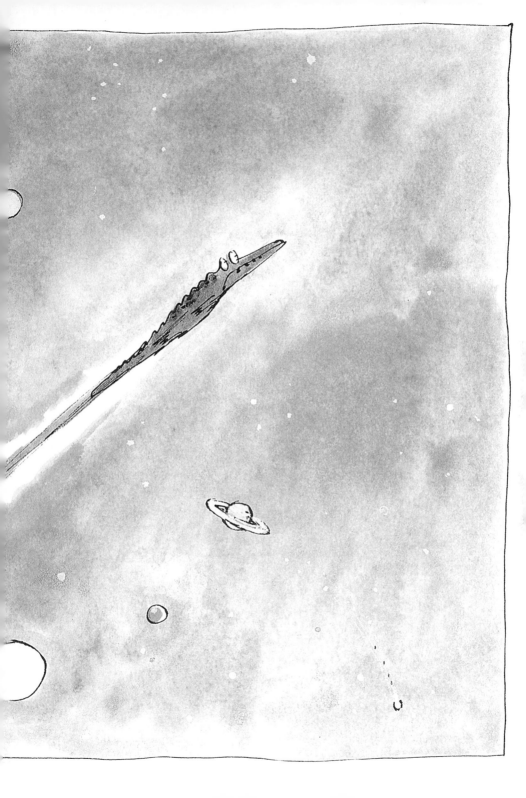

He whizzed[39] on and on.

He whizzed far into space.

He whizzed past the moon.

He whizzed past stars and planets.

Until at last ...

With the most tremendous

BANG!

the Enormous Crocodile crashed

headfirst into the hot hot sun.

And he was sizzled[40] up like a sausage!

查單字

1 Enormous Crocodile：達爾專用字。意指體型超級無敵大的鱷魚。

2 Notsobig One：達爾專用字。指體型沒那麼大的另一隻鱷魚。

3 gollop：（口語）指狼吞虎嚥的吃東西。此處達爾用來形容咕嚕一口吞下去。

4 tommy-rot：荒唐；極為愚蠢。

5 Humpy-Rumpy：此處達爾專指河馬的名字「俏翹臀」。

hump：圓形隆起物；駝峰。

rump：臀部。

6 on earth：究竟；到底。

7 grumptious：（口語）為「grumpy」的另一個用 法，

形容脾氣暴躁。此處達爾用來形容鱷魚的殘暴。

8 waddle：蹣跚而行；搖擺而行。

9 Trunky：形容壯碩、沒有腰身。此處達爾專指大象的名字壯壯鼻。

10 foul：令人厭惡的；有惡臭的；汙穢的；邪惡的；粗鄙的。

11 filthy：骯髒的；邪惡的；汙穢的。

12 fiend：惡魔；窮凶極惡之人。

13 squash：壓爛；壓扁；壓壞；壓擠；壓縮

14 squish：（口語）此處達爾形容鱷魚的骨頭被擠碎而發出嘎吱聲。

15 squizzle：（口語）意思是被用力抱住而喘不過氣。此處也是達爾形容鱷魚被用力擠壓的意思。

16 Muggle-Wump：在此達爾是指猴子的名字麻果昂波。

麻果昂波在《壞心的夫妻消失了》被刁先生和刁太太關在大籠子裡。一般認為哈利波特中的「麻瓜」（Muggle）一詞源自於此。

mugwump：中立者，騎牆派。或指大人物或印第安酋長。

mug：（口語）意指鬼臉。

17 hoggish：貪婪而自私的。

18 Roly-Poly：指加了果醬、水果等的布丁捲，或形容矮胖、圓滾滾的。在此達爾是指鳥的名字布丁捲鳥。布丁捲鳥後來在《壞心的夫妻消失了》一書中拯救了麻果昂波一家人和許多的小鳥。

19 luscious：味道與氣味甜美的；動人的。

20 mushious：源自於「mush」，原意為軟糊狀食物，但達爾特地使用「mushious」達成押韻效果。

21 duper：意思是「很棒的」，比「super」的程度更高一級。達爾在第一行及第二行以 super 及 duper 結尾作押韻效果，並有強調超級好吃的意味在其中。英美人士喜歡在談笑時以「super-duper」強調「有多棒」，但不適合一本正經的使用。

22 mash：搗成糊狀。

23 munch：津津有味的咀嚼。

24 crunch：嘎吱作響的咬嚼。

25 squish：發出嘎吱聲。

★ mash、munch、crunch、squish 都是達爾刻意強調

大快朵頤，並有押韻的趣味效果。

26 whoosh：東西飛快移動的聲音。

27 gallop：奔馳；飛跑。

28 tumble：跌倒；滾動；摔落。

29 skid：原意為打滑；滑向一側。

原文 skidding over the ground 表示鱷魚越過地面上方滑出去，以現在年輕世代的口吻，相當於「被踹飛」或「被撞飛」的意思。

30 bag：袋子；獵獲物；占據（口語）。

31 knobbly：有圓形突起物的；有節的；有疙瘩的；有球塊的。

32 dodgem-car：電動碰碰車。

33 candy-floss：棉花糖。

　floss：亂絲；絲棉。

34 roundabout：旋轉木馬。

35 flock：聚集；成群的來或去。

36 swish：作窸窣聲；沙沙的響；發出颼颼聲的移動。

37 swoosh：颼颼聲；發出颼颼聲。

　★ swish 和 swoosh 是達爾強調布丁捲鳥揮動翅膀、穿越森林飛行的聲音，有音韻上的趣味效果。

38 swizzle：原意為過量喝酒。此處達爾用以描述旋轉、轉動。

39 whiz：物體掠過空中的聲音；咻咻急馳掠過。

40 sizzle：把……燒得發出嘶嘶聲。

羅爾德 · 達爾

出生：1916 年於英國威爾斯地德蘭道夫誕生。

學歷：雷普敦聖彼得市德蘭道夫天主教學校。

職業：殼牌石油公司東非代表。第二次世界大戰英
　　　國皇家空軍戰鬥機飛行員，空軍武官，作家。

正如《長頸鹿、小鵜兒和我》故事中的比利一樣，羅爾德 · 達爾一直夢想著擁有一間自己的糖果店。他特別喜愛巧克力，而且曉得跟巧克力有關的每一件事。他和朋友們還是學生時，偶爾會受邀當開德堡瑞斯巧克力試吃員，他便對巧克力著迷了。

達爾居住在大密森頓德吉普賽屋時，每一頓飯後都會

拿出一個裝著各種不同口味巧克力的紅色塑膠盒與每個人分享。

1990 年去世，享年七十四歲。

你可以到羅爾德 · 達爾的網站上尋找更多與他有關的事情：www.roalddahl.com

羅爾德·達爾
不只說精采的故事⋯⋯

你知道嗎？本書作者版稅的 10% 會捐給
羅爾德·達爾慈善機構嗎？

● 羅爾達·達爾優良兒童慈善機構（Roald Dahl's Marvellous Children's Charity）：羅爾德·達爾以故事和韻文聞名，但鮮為人知的是，他其實常常幫助罹患重症的兒童。所以現在羅爾達·達爾優良兒童慈善機構秉承他不凡的善行，幫助數以千計罹患神經或血液相關疾病的孩童，以期接近達爾善良的心。此機構也為英國孩童提供護理照料、醫療設備，以及很重要的——娛樂，並透過先驅研究幫助世界各地的孩童。

你願意拿出實際行動來幫助別人嗎？

詳情請看：www.roalddahlcharity.org。

●羅爾德・達爾博物館暨故事中心（Roald Dahl Museum and Story Centre）：設立於倫敦郊外的白金漢郡大密森頓市，也是羅爾德・達爾生前居住與寫作的地方。達爾的信件與手稿展示於博物館的中心位置；另外還有兩間展示達爾生平、充滿童趣的展覽室：一間互動式的故事中心，以及他著名的寫作小屋。

羅爾達・達爾優良兒童慈善機構為正式註冊的慈善團體，登記字號為1137409。
羅爾德・達爾博物館暨故事中心為正式註冊的慈善團體，登記字號為1085853。
羅爾德・達爾信託基金（The Roald Dahl Charitable Trust）為新成立的慈善機構，以支援上列二個團體的運作。
*註：版稅捐款已扣除佣金。

國家圖書館出版品預行編目資料

大大大大的鱷魚 / 羅爾德‧達爾（Roald Dahl）著；
昆丁‧布雷克（Quentin Blake）繪；顏銘新譯. --
二版 . --台北市：幼獅，2013.07
　面；　公分. --（故事館；8）
譯自：The Enormous Crocodile
ISBN 978-957-574-909-5（平裝）

873.59　　　　　　　　　　102008725

‧故事館008‧

大大大大的鱷魚

作　　　者＝羅爾德‧達爾（Roald Dahl）
繪　　　圖＝昆丁‧布雷克（Quentin Blake）
譯　　　者＝顏銘新
出 版 者＝幼獅文化事業股份有限公司
發 行 人＝葛永光
總 經 理＝王華金
總 編 輯＝林碧琪
主　　　編＝沈怡汝
編　　　輯＝白宜平
美術編輯＝游巧鈴
總 公 司＝10045台北市重慶南路1段66-1號3樓
電　　　話＝(02)2311-2832
傳　　　真＝(02)2311-5368
郵政劃撥＝00033368

印　　　刷＝崇寶彩藝印刷股份有限公司
定　　　價＝200元
港　　　幣＝67元
二　　　版＝2013.07
二　　　刷＝2022.09
書　　　號＝987206

幼獅樂讀網
http://www.youth.com.tw
幼獅購物網
http://shopping.youth.com.tw
e-mail:customer@youth.com.tw

行政院新聞局核准登記證局版台業字第0143號
有著作權‧侵害必究(若有缺頁或破損，請寄回更換)
欲利用本書內容者，請洽幼獅公司圖書組(02)2314-6001#234

幼獅文化公司 ／讀者服務卡／

感謝您購買幼獅公司出版的好書！

為提升服務品質與出版更優質的圖書，敬請撥冗填寫後（免貼郵票）擲寄本公司，或傳真（傳真電話02-23115368），我們將參考您的意見、分享您的觀點，出版更多的好書。並不定期提供您相關書訊、活動、特惠專案等。謝謝！

基本資料

姓名：＿＿＿＿＿＿＿＿＿＿＿＿先生／小姐

婚姻狀況：□已婚 □未婚　職業：□學生 □公教 □上班族 □家管 □其他

出生：民國＿＿＿＿年＿＿＿＿月＿＿＿＿日

電話：（公）＿＿＿＿（宅）＿＿＿＿（手機）＿＿＿＿

e-mail：＿＿＿＿

聯絡地址：＿＿＿＿

1.您所購買的書名：　**大大大大的鱷魚**

2.您通常以何種方式購書?：□1.書店買書 □2.網路購書 □3.傳真訂購 □4.郵局劃撥
（可複選）　　□5.幼獅門市 □6.團體訂購 □7.其他

3.您是否曾買過幼獅其他出版品：□是，□1.圖書 □2.幼獅文藝 □3.幼獅少年
□否

4.您從何處得知本書訊息：□1.師長介紹 □2.朋友介紹 □3.幼獅少年雜誌
（可複選）　　□4.幼獅文藝雜誌 □5.報章雜誌書評介紹＿＿＿＿報
□6.DM傳單、海報 □7.書店 □8.廣播(　　)
□9.電子報、edm □10.其他

5.您喜歡本書的原因：□1.作者 □2.書名 □3.內容 □4.封面設計 □5.其他

6.您不喜歡本書的原因：□1.作者 □2.書名 □3.內容 □4.封面設計 □5.其他

7.您希望得知的出版訊息：□1.青少年讀物 □2.兒童讀物 □3.親子叢書
□4.教師充電系列 □5.其他

8.您覺得本書的價格：□1.偏高 □2.合理 □3.偏低

9.讀完本書後您覺得：□1.很有收穫 □2.有收穫 □3.收穫不多 □4.沒收穫

10.敬請推薦親友，共同加入我們的閱讀計畫，我們將適時寄送相關書訊，以豐富書香與心靈的空間：

(1)姓名＿＿＿＿e-mail＿＿＿＿電話＿＿＿＿

(2)姓名＿＿＿＿e-mail＿＿＿＿電話＿＿＿＿

(3)姓名＿＿＿＿e-mail＿＿＿＿電話＿＿＿＿

11.您對本書或本公司的建議：

10045　台北市重慶南路一段66-1號3樓

幼獅文化事業股份有限公司

請沿虛線對折寄回

客服專線：02-23112832分機208　傳真：02-23115368

e-mail：customer@youth.com.tw

幼獅樂讀網http：//www.youth.com.tw